A Piñata in a Pine Tree

A Latino Twelve Days of Christmas

By Pat Mora

Illustrated by Magaly Morales

Clarion Books

Houghton Mifflin Harcourt

Boston ★ New York

2009

Clarion Books ✳ 3 Park Avenue, 19th Floor, New York, NY 10016 ✳ Text copyright © 2009 by Pat Mora ✳ Illustrations copyright © 2009 by Magaly Morales ✳ The illustrations were executed in acrylics. ✳ The text was set in 16-point Formata. ✳ All rights reserved. ✳ For information about permission to reproduce selections from this book, write to Permissions, Houghton Mifflin Harcourt Publishing Company, 3 Park Avenue, 19th Floor, New York, NY 10016. ✳ Clarion Books is an imprint of Houghton Mifflin Harcourt Publishing Company. ✳ www.clarionbooks.com ✳ Printed in Malaysia ✳ *Library of Congress Cataloging-in-Publication Data* ✳ Mora, Pat. ✳ A piñata in a pine tree : a Latino twelve days of Christmas / by Pat Mora. ✳ p. cm. ✳ Summary: In this adaptation of the folk song "The Twelve Days of Christmas," friends exchange such gifts as a piñata and "cuatro luminarias." Includes pronunciation and glossary of Spanish words and a description of Christmas foods and other holiday traditions from different Latin American countries. ✳ ISBN 978-0-618-84198-1 ✳ 1. Children's songs—United States—Texts. 2. Christmas music—Texts. [1. Latin Americans—Songs and music. 2. Christmas music. 3. Songs.] I. Twelve days of Christmas (English folk song) II. Title. ✳ PZ8.3.M794Pin 2009 ✳ 782.42'1723—dc22 [E] ✳ 2008032463 TWP 10 9 8 7   4500763395

On the first day of Christmas, my amiga gave to me

a *piñata* in a pine tree.

4

On the second day of

Christmas, my *amiga* gave to me

pah·stel·EE·tohs

dos pastelitos and
a *piñata* in a pine tree.

2

dohs

On the third day of Christmas, my amiga gave to me

trehs

3

tres tamalitos,
dos pastelitos, and
a piñata in a pine tree.

8

tah·mahl·EE·tohs

9

On the fourth day of Christmas, my amiga gave to me

cuatro luminarias,
tres tamalitos,
dos pastelitos, and
a piñata in a pine tree.

10

loo·meen·AHR·ee·ahs

koo·WAH·troh

11

ghee·tahr EE·tahs

On the fifth day of Christmas, my amiga gave to me

cinco guitarritas,
cuatro luminarias,
tres tamalitos,
dos pastelitos, and
a piñata in a pine tree.

On the sixth day of Christmas, my amiga gave to me

seis trompos girando,
cinco guitarritas,
cuatro luminarias,
tres tamalitos,
dos pastelitos, and
a piñata in a pine tree.

6 SAYS

TROHM·pohs
hee·RAHN·doh

15

On the seventh day of Christmas, my amiga gave to me

siete burritos bailando,
seis trompos girando,
cinco guitarritas,
cuatro luminarias,
tres tamalitos,
dos pastelitos, and
a *piñata* in a pine tree.

boo·REE·tohs by·LAHN·doh

16

see·EH·teh

On the eighth day of Christmas, my amiga gave to me

ocho pajaritos serenando,
siete burritos bailando,
seis trompos girando,
cinco guitarritas,
cuatro luminarias,
tres tamalitos,
dos pastelitos, and
a piñata in a pine tree.

OH · choh

18

19

On the ninth day of Christmas, my amiga gave to me

nueve campanitas sonando,
ocho pajaritos serenando,
siete burritos bailando,
seis trompos girando,
cinco guitarritas,
cuatro luminarias,
tres tamalitos,
dos pastelitos, and
a *piñata* in a pine tree.

cahm · pahn · EE · tahs
soh · NAHN · doh

20

noo·EH·veh

9

On the tenth day of Christmas, my amiga gave to me

diez estrellitas saltando,
nueve campanitas sonando,
ocho pajaritos serenando,
siete burritos bailando,
seis trompos girando,
cinco guitarritas,
cuatro luminarias,
tres tamalitos,
dos pastelitos, and
a piñata in a pine tree.

10

dee·ehs

ehs-treh-YEE-tahs
sahl-TAHN-doh

23

On the eleventh day of Christmas, my amiga gave to me

once lunitas cantando,
diez estrellitas saltando,
nueve campanitas sonando,
ocho pajaritos serenando,
siete burritos bailando,
seis trompos girando,
cinco guitarritas,
cuatro luminarias,
tres tamalitos,
dos pastelitos, and
a *piñata* in a pine tree.

DOH·seh

ahn·jeh·LEE·tohs
sell·eh·BRAHN·doh

Ah, my amiga!

On the twelfth day of Christmas, my amiga gave to me

doce angelitos celebrando,
once lunitas cantando,
diez estrellitas saltando,
nueve campanitas sonando,
ocho pajaritos serenando,
siete burritos bailando,
seis trompos girando,
cinco guitarritas,
cuatro luminarias,
tres tamalitos,
dos pastelitos, and
a piñata in a pine tree.

Glossary and Pronunciation Guide

NUMBERS

*uno (OO-noh): one

dos (dohs): two

tres (trehs): three

cuatro (koo-WAH-troh): four

cinco (SEEN-coh): five

seis (says): six

siete (see-EH-teh): seven

ocho (OH-choh): eight

nueve (noo-EH-veh): nine

diez (dee-ehs): ten

once (OHN-seh): eleven

doce (DOH-seh): twelve

In Spanish, the ending -itos or -itas connotes both the diminutive and a tone of affection often used when speaking to children.

WORDS

amiga (ah-MEE-gah): friend

piñata (pee-NYAH-tah): small clay pot decorated with colored paper

pastelitos (pah-stel-EE-tohs): small pies or turnovers

tamalitos (tah-mahl-EE-tohs): corn dough filled with cooked meat or chicken wrapped in corn husks and steamed

luminarias (loo-meen-AHR-ee-ahs): paper lanterns

guitarritas (ghee-tahr-EE-tahs): guitars

trompos girando (TROHM-pohs hee-RAHN-doh): spinning tops

burritos bailando (boo-REE-tohs by-LAHN-doh): dancing donkeys

pajaritos serenando (pah-hah-REE-tohs seh-rehn-AHN-doh): serenading birds

campanitas sonando (cahm-pahn-EE tahs soh-NAHN-doh): bells ringing

estrellitas saltando (ehs-treh-YEE-tahs sahl-THAN-doh): stars skipping

lunitas cantando (loo-NEE-tahs cahn-THAN-doh): singing moons

angelitos celebrando (ahn-jeh-LEE-tohs sell-eh-BRAHN-doh): angels rejoicing

* When paired with a feminine noun such as *piñata*, *uno* becomes *una*. When paired with a masculine noun, *uno* becomes *un*.

Author's Note

One of the pleasures of being a Latina born in the United States is that I grew up with Mexican holiday traditions as well as singing the Christmas carols popular in the United States. Although most people are familiar with the song "The Twelve Days of Christmas," many are not aware that the twelve days begin on Christmas Day and end January 5, twelfth night, the night before Epiphany, or the Feast of the Three Kings. This holiday is more widely celebrated in Latin America than in the United States. In *A Piñata in a Pine Tree*, I've enjoyed blending both worlds.

In addition to music, one of the joys of Christmas is, of course, food. In the southwestern United States, *pastelitos,* usually in the shape of turnovers, contain sweet fillings—apricot, apple, or cherry. In other countries, including Cuba and the Dominican Republic, the turnovers are filled with beef or chicken. *Tamales* are often prepared at Christmas as well: masa, a cornmeal dough, is spread on clean cornhusks and filled with cooked beef or chicken, or sometimes chile peppers. The tamales are then wrapped and steamed. In Mexico, sweet tamales often contain raisins, nuts, and anise flavorings. In Central American countries, such as El Salvador and Honduras, and in Peru, tamales are wrapped in banana leaves instead of cornhusks.

Luminarias, another Latino tradition, are lights, hanging lights, or paper lanterns, called *farolitos* in New Mexico. On Christmas Eve, especially in the southwestern United States, small brown paper bags are filled partway with sand to keep them upright, and then a small candle is placed inside. Luminarias symbolize lighting the way for the Christ Child.

Many of the other gifts in this book were inspired by Mexican tree ornaments made out of tin—including bells, suns, stars, moons, birds, animals, and angels. These ornaments fill museums and store windows and shelves at Christmas in Sante Fe, New Mexico, where I now live. My three children, though grown now, still look forward to hanging our own familiar tin donkey and bell ornaments. In fact, I use some of these ornaments all year round in my kitchen.

I hope you enjoy singing this new version of "The Twelve Days of Christmas" and perhaps will be inspired to create new lyrics based on your own family traditions.

Illustrator's Note

The illustrations for this book were made with acrylic paint in a *fiesta* of color, light, shadow, and detail to celebrate this most joyous of holidays. In Mexico, where I live, the twelve days of Christmas begin December 26 and end January 6, with the arrival of *Los Reyes Magos* (the Three Wise Men), who bring gifts for the children. In *A Piñata in a Pine Tree,* the narrator's secret *amiga* leaves her gifts each of the twelve days. If all the gifts were added up, they would total 364, almost one for every day of the year. If they were all to appear in the illustrations, they would overflow the pages! That is why only the new gifts for each day are shown: *uno* on the first day, *dos* on the second, and so on. I tried to give each of the twelve gifts a traditional Mexican flavor as well as a magical feel. For instance, the donkeys dancing in the air are modeled after intricate keepsake figures handwoven from strips of palm leaves that are popular in Veracruz, Mexico. But my favorite are the little angels that on the twelfth day announce the joyful arrival of the best present of all: a beautiful sister, a new *amiga.*

A Piñata in a Pine Tree

On the first day of Christ - mas, my a - mi - ga gave to me a pi - ña - ta___ in a pine

tree. 2. On the sec - ond day of Christ - mas, my a - mi - ga gave to me
3. On the third___ day of Christ - mas, my a - mi - ga gave to me
4. On the fourth___ day of Christ - mas, my a - mi - ga gave to me

Repeat as needed

D.S. for Verses 3-4

dos___ pas - te - li - tos, and a pi - ña - ta___ in a pine tree. On the
tres___ ta - mal - i - tos,
cua - tro lu - mi - na - ri - as,

fifth day of Christ mas, my a - mi - ga gave to me cin - co gui - ta - rri - tas,

cua - tro lu - mi - na - ri - as, tres ta - ma - li - tos, dos___ pas - te - li - tos, and a pi -

Fine

ña - ta___ in a pine tree. 6. On the sixth___ day of Christ - mas, my a - mi - ga gave to me

* see below for Verses 7-12

Repeat as needed for Verses 7-12

To ⊕ for Verses 7-12

seis___ trom - pos gi - ran - do, cin - co gui - ta - rri - tas,

To Fine after Verse 12

* 7. On the seventh day of Christmas,
my amiga gave to me
siete burritos bailando,
seis trompos . . .

8. On the eighth day of Christmas,
my amiga gave to me
ocho pajaritos serenando,
siete burritos . . .

9. On the ninth day of Christmas,
my amiga gave to me
nueve campanitas sonando,
ocho pajaritos . . .

10. On the tenth day of Christmas,
my amiga gave to me
diez estrellitas saltando,
nueve campanitas . . .

11. On the eleventh day of Christmas,
my amiga gave to me
once lunitas cantando,
diez estrellitas . . .

12. On the twelfth day of Christmas,
my amiga gave to me
doce angelitos celebrando,
once lunitas . . .

Please note, some of the later verses have more than one syllable per note.